Pokémon™

AWESOME EVOLUTIONS!

BY C. J. NESTOR

A Random House PICTUREBACK® Book

Random House 🏠 New York

© 2019 The Pokémon Company International. © 1995–2019 Nintendo / Creatures Inc.
/ GAME FREAK inc. TM, ®, and character names are trademarks of Nintendo.
Published in the United States by Random House Children's Books, a division of
Penguin Random House LLC, 1745 Broadway, New York, NY 10019, and in Canada
by Penguin Random House Canada Limited, Toronto. Pictureback, Random House, and the
Random House colophon are registered trademarks of Penguin Random House LLC.
ISBN 978-1-9848-4830-7
rhcbooks.com
MANUFACTURED IN CHINA
10 9 8 7 6 5 4 3 2 1
Glow effect and production: Red Bird Publishing Ltd., U.K.

P9-BXY-598

Hello! My name is **PROFESSOR OAK**. I'm one of the leading experts on Pokémon in the world. Something I love about Pokémon is how they grow when you partner with them. Through training, traveling, and growing as friends with Pokémon, Trainers can watch their Pokémon develop in incredible ways!

There are many methods by which Pokémon evolve. Some, like **LILLIPUP**, evolve with lots of training and hard work. Others evolve through contact with mysterious items, visiting a particular place, or the friendship with their Trainers.

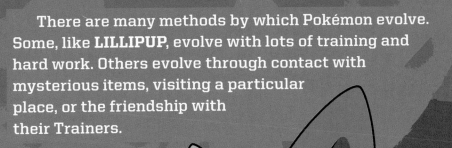

Lillipup can evolve into **HERDIER**, and Herdier can evolve into **STOUTLAND**.

Let's take a look at some amazing Pokémon evolutions!

We'll start with **PIKACHU**.

The Tiny Mouse Pokémon **PICHU** evolves into Pikachu. Pichu is not as powerful as Pikachu, and it isn't as good at controlling its electric shocks, either, so sometimes it will shock its Trainer or even itself!

A very close bond between a Pichu and its Trainer might allow the Pichu to evolve!

For Pikachu to evolve into **RAICHU**, it needs a Thunder Stone—one of the mysterious objects that can affect certain Pokémon.

If Pikachu evolves while in Alola, it will evolve into the Electric- and Psychic-type **ALOLAN RAICHU**, rather than the Electric-type Raichu seen elsewhere. It's not known why some Alolan Pokémon look different from other Pokémon of the same species, but it might be due to the Pokémon's diet.

Another Pokémon with an interesting evolution path is **VULPIX**. This Fire-type Pokémon's tails keep splitting as it grows.

When Vulpix is exposed to a Fire Stone, it becomes **NINETALES** and can live for a thousand years and bend any flame to its will. According to legend, Ninetales was created when nine saints merged into a single being.

Not all Vulpix and Ninetales look the same, though!
Coming from the mountains of Alola, these Vulpix are
Ice-type Pokémon, rather than Fire-type.

ALOLAN VULPIX uses a spray of ice crystals from its coat to stay cool,
but when it evolves into **ALOLAN NINETALES**, that ice spray becomes a
fearsome weapon that can freeze opponents in their tracks!

RALTS has a fascinating evolutionary path. This Psychic- and Fairy-type Pokémon uses the horns on its head to sense people's emotions, and it is drawn to people with a positive attitude to be its Trainer.

With some training, Ralts evolves into **KIRLIA**, a Pokémon with psychic powers that can produce strange mirages.

Kirlia can evolve in one of two ways. With time and effort, it can evolve into **GARDEVOIR**, a powerful Psychic- and Fairy-type Pokémon that can see the future and defend its Trainer with its psychic powers.

However, if a male Kirlia is exposed to a Dawn Stone, it will evolve into **GALLADE!** This Pokémon is both a Fighting- and a Psychic-type and is a master swordfighter, using its elbows like blades.

This Fish Pokémon, **MAGIKARP**, is not the best to have in battle—but with patience and a lot of training, it can evolve into the astoundingly destructive **GYARADOS**.

While Magikarp is known to simply splash in place, Gyarados has a fearsome temper!

FEEBAS might not be a beautiful Pokémon, but it is hardy and can live comfortably in the dirtiest water. With a lot of encouragement from its Trainer, a Feebas that feels beautiful can evolve into a **MILOTIC**.

Milotic is so lovely that some artists search far and wide to find one and capture its beauty in their works!

EEVEE is one of the most fascinating Pokémon you'll find when it comes to evolution. According to our current knowledge, this amazing little one can evolve into no fewer than eight different Pokémon!

Even more interesting is the fact that Eevee doesn't always evolve in the same way! In certain cases, Eevee can evolve when it touches a specific type of Evolution stone, or when it is close to a particular rock, such as a Mossy Rock or an Ice Rock.

Otherwise, if Eevee bonds with its Trainer, the time of day or night may govern its evolution. And an Eevee's close, affectionate relationship with its Trainer sometimes affects its evolution, too! No wonder Eevee is called the Evolution Pokémon!

If you are looking for perseverance, look no further than the Rock Head Pokémon, **BAGON**. It jumps and tries its hardest to fly, and when it grows frustrated, it smashes things with its powerful head!

With intense training, it can evolve into **SHELGON**, and though it appears to be completely motionless, the changes going on inside this Pokémon's hard shell allow it to evolve into **SALAMENCE**, the Dragon Pokémon.

Salamence is so happy to finally be able to fly that it gets a little overexcited—but can you blame it?

TYROGUE is so fierce about its training, it becomes stressed out if it doesn't get to train every day. When it is ready, it can evolve into three different Pokémon!

A well-trained Tyrogue can evolve into **HITMONCHAN**, the Punching Pokémon, which will never stop trying to become a champion.

Tyrogue can also evolve into **HITMONTOP**, the Handstand Pokémon, whose unique fighting style of spinning kicks at high speed makes it strong in all aspects of battle.

Another possible evolution is **HITMONLEE**, the Kicking Pokémon, which uses its powerful legs like springs, delivering kick after kick until it knocks its opponent out.

Now, these Pokémon are really worth a look! They might seem to be completely different, but **SHELMET**, the Snail Pokémon, and **KARRABLAST**, the Clamping Pokémon, have a connection beyond Karrablast's desire to steal Shelmet's shell.

When electrical energy surrounds them at the same time, something amazing happens!

Upon evolving, Shelmet sheds its shell and becomes **ACCELGOR**. Free of that heavy weight, Accelgor is then able to dart around the battlefield and attack from all directions.

Meanwhile, Karrablast uses the shell from Shelmet to evolve into **ESCAVALIER**, defending itself while it attacks with its two new lances.

Around the islands of Alola, **ROCKRUFF** is a very common Pokémon to see with new Trainers. It is a friendly Pokémon, although it tends to develop a bit of a wild streak as it grows. Rockruff evolves into **LYCANROC**, and this Wolf Pokémon's **MIDDAY FORM** is fiercely loyal to the Trainer who has raised it kindly.

Rockruff can also evolve into the MIDNIGHT FORM of Lycanroc. This form attacks recklessly, using the hard rocks in its mane to perform crushing head-butts.

Rarely, a Rockruff will evolve into the DUSK FORM of Lycanroc. This Pokémon is both calm and fierce. No one is sure what causes the evolution into Lycanroc's Dusk Form! However, it might have something to do with the green flash sometimes seen at sunset.

Be careful not to hold **HONEDGE**, a Steel- and Ghost-type Pokémon, like the sword it resembles. When it evolves into **DOUBLADE**, it divides into two swords that fight together in bewildering slash patterns. Doublade can also evolve into **AEGISLASH**, the Royal Pokémon. Records say that this Pokémon used to accompany kings and queens in years past.

Finally, we reach a new discovery, one I am quite excited about—a Legendary Pokémon that evolves! We aren't sure where **COSMOG** originates, although some researchers think it may have come from another world. It grows by gathering dust from the atmosphere, which is possibly why it's sometimes referred to as the Child of the Stars!

Cosmog evolves into **COSMOEM**, which never moves, although inside its hard outer cocoon, massive changes are occurring.

Eventually, Cosmoem will evolve into either the Sunne Pokémon, **SOLGALEO**, or the Moone Pokémon, **LUNALA**! What a spectacular sight that must be! Solgaleo's light is said to banish the deepest darkness. while Lunala can turn midday to midnight.

There are always new discoveries to be made! What still lies out there? I'm excited to find out!